6/12

Quantum Boogaloo

HEY, FERB. WHAT DO YOU CALL IT WHEN YOU BUMP INTO YOURSELF IN THE FUTURE?

ADAPTED BY JOHN GREEN

BASED ON THE SERIES CREATED BY
DAN POVENMIRE & JEFF "SWAMPY" MARSH

DISNEP PRESS
NEW YORK

ISBN 978-1-4231-3739-9
FIRST EDITION
10 9 8 7 6 5 4 3 2 1
PRINTED IN THE UNITED STATES OF AMERICA
H886-4759-0-11130

FOR MORE DISNEY PRESS FUN, VISIT WWW.DISNEYBOOKS.COM
VISIT DISNEYCHANNEL.COM

GRAPH
GREEN

SUMMER VACATION! THERE'S A WHOLE LOT OF STUFF TO DO BEFORE SCHOOL STARTS, AND **PHINEAS** AND **FERB** PLAN TO DO IT ALL! MAYBE THEY'LL BUILD A ROCKET, OR FIND FRANKENSTEIN'S BRAIN...WHATEVER THEY DO, THEY'RE SURE TO ANNOY THEIR SISTER, **CANDACE.** MEANWHILE, THEIR FAMILY PET, **PERRY** THE PLATYPUS, LEADS A DOUBLE LIFE AS **AGENT P,** FACING OFF AGAINST THE DEVIOUS **DR. DOOFENSHMIRTZ!**

QUANTUM BOOGALOO

WELL, WE'VE FINISHED THE SUPERSTRUCTURE, BUT WHAT WE REALLY NEED NOW IS A *TOOL* THAT WILL FUSE WOOD AND METAL AT A MOLECULAR LEVEL.

ANY IDEAS, BALJEET?

TECHNOLOGY LIKE *THAT* IS TWENTY YEARS AWAY, PHINEAS. YOU WOULD NEED A *TIME MACHINE.* LUCKILY, I HAVE BEEN WORKING ON A DESIGN. I HAVE NOT FIGURED OUT ALL THE QUANTUM PHYSICS YET, BUT IF YOU GIVE ME A COUPLE OF DAYS--

OR WE COULD JUST USE THE ONE AT THE MUSEUM.

THERE IS A TIME MACHINE AT THE MUSEUM?

YEAH, WE TOOK IT BACK TO THE *MESOZOIC ERA.*

YOU GOT TO HANG OUT WITH DINOSAURS?

YEAH, EARLIER THIS SUMMER.

HMPH!

WELL, *THANK YOU* FOR INVITING ME.

FERB, I KNOW WHAT WE'RE GONNA DO TODAY. OR I *SHOULD* SAY, I KNOW WHAT WE'RE GONNA DO *TWENTY YEARS* FROM TODAY.

HEY, GUYS. WHAT'CHA DOIN'?

CAN I COME?

WE'RE TIME TRAVELING.

WHY NOT?

MEANWHILE...

YEAH STACY, THEY'RE BUILDING SOMETHING OUT THERE. BUT I'VE DECIDED THE PROBLEM IS I ALWAYS JUMP THE GUN, SO I'M GONNA WAIT 'TIL JUST THE *RIGHT* MOMENT TO--

CANDACE? HELLO?

THEY'RE ON THE MOVE. I'LL BUST 'EM NOW! *I'LL BUST 'EM NOW!*

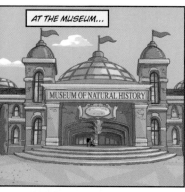

AT THE MUSEUM...

MUSEUM OF NATURAL HISTORY

TWENTY YEARS FORWARD, AND AWAY WE *GO!*

ZZAPP!

SO *THAT'S* IT! THEY'RE TIME TRAVELING AGAIN. AND THE BEST PART IS THEY HAVE TO RETURN TO THIS *EXACT* SPOT. AND I'LL BE STANDING *RIGHT HERE* WITH MOM TO BUST THEM WHEN THEY DO!

ACTUALLY, RIGHT OVER *HERE.* I'D BE CRUSHED BY THE MACHINE IF I WAS STANDING THERE.

AAAND I'M TALKING TO NOBODY.

TWENTY YEARS IN THE FUTURE...

ZZAPP!

HERE WE ARE, TWENTY YEARS IN THE FUTURE!

ISABELLA, YOU WAIT HERE; YOU'RE THE ONLY ONE WE CAN TRUST TO WATCH THE MACHINE.

HE TRUSTS ME.

Clank!

OOPS!

4

ZZAP!

EHH, I HATED CLEANING THAT THING ANYWAY.

THE BOYS HEAD OUT TO EXPLORE FUTURE DANVILLE...

MUSEUM OF NATURAL HIST

I SEE THE MUSEUM FINALLY ADDED THAT NEW WING.

AND WOULD YOU LOOK HOW *DANVILLE'S* CHANGED!

FLYING CARS! JET PACKS!

HEY, LOOK AT THAT! THAT LOOKS LIKE-- *IT IS!*

IT'S *CANDACE* TWENTY YEARS OLDER! I ALMOST DIDN'T RECOGNIZE HER; SHE LOOKS SO *RELAXED.*

AND *THOSE* MUST BE HER KIDS IN THE YARD.

MOM! XAVIER AND FRED ARE DOING NOTHING AGAIN!

I CAN'T BELIEVE YOU, XAVIER AND FRED. YOU TWO ARE SO *LAZY.* IT'S SUMMER VACATION, AND YOU'RE *WASTING* IT! YOU GUYS NEVER DO *ANYTHING!*

I'M SITTING UNDER THIS DIGITAL TREE.

I'M SITTING NEXT TO HIM.

zzt!

HI GUYS. WHAT'CHA DOIN'?

I'M SITTING UNDER THIS DIGITAL TREE.

I'M SITTING NEXT TO HIM.

OH, STACY, *EVERY* JOB HAS ITS PROBLEMS, BUT THERE'S GOTTA BE AN UPSIDE TO BEING PRESIDENT OF URUGUAY. NO, HUH? ME? I'M FINE, THE KIDS ARE FINE. XAVIER AND FRED ARE IN THE BACKYARD WITH THE YOUNG PHINEAS AND FERB.

YOUNG PHINEAS AND FERB?!

GOTTA GO, STA GOOD LUCK WITH LLAMA LEGISLA

AND YESTERDAY I WAS SITTING ON THE LEFT.

AND I WAS SITTING NEXT TO HIM.

ON THE RIGHT. WE LIKE TO MIX IT UP.

IT *IS* THEM!

I BET THEY TRAVELED HERE FROM THE PAST.

AW, LOOK HOW *CUTE* AND *BUST-ABLE* THEY LOOK!

WAIT-- ISN'T THIS JUST A *DIGITAL* TREE?

ZZT!

AAAAHH!

FWUMP!

HEY, MOM.

HI, CANDACE.

AAAAAHH!!

I'M TELLING MOM!

HEY. THAT REMINDS ME. WHERE'S PERRY?

MEANWHILE, AT DOOFENSHMIRTZ EVIL, INC...

I'VE *FINALLY* GOT YOU, PERRY THE PLATYPUS.

Doofenshmirtz Evil Inc.

THE *ENDGAME* IS FINALLY HERE.

OH, WAIT. I-I MOVED THE WRONG PIECE.

-:SNORE:-

I'LL JUST MOVE IT BACK...

-:SNORE:-

-:SNOR--

?

SPLOOSH

CHOMP!

AAAAHH!!

AAAAHH!!

DOO-BE DOO-BE DO-BA...

-:WHEEZE:-

...DOO-BE DOO-BE DO-BA!

-:WHEEEEEEZE:-

SO, WHAT SPECTACULAR ADVENTURES HAVE YOU GOT LINED UP FOR THIS SUMMER?

I'M SITTING UNDER THIS DIGITAL TREE.

AND I'M SITTING NEXT TO HIM.

THAT'S *IT*? BUT IT'S SUMMER VACATION! AND YOU'RE FREE TO DO *ANYTHING*.

YEAH, BUT THIS IS THE *FUTURE.* EVERYTHING'S ALREADY BEEN DONE.

THE STONE AGE WAS ONCE THE *FUTURE.* AS WAS THE MIDDLE AGES. CREATIVITY AND INVENTION *NEVER* END!

SO, WHAT ARE YOU GUYS GONNA MAKE THIS SUMMER?

HOW 'BOUT BUMPER CARS THAT MOVE IN FIVE DIMENSIONS?

OH, YEAH. OKAY. WE'LL DO *THAT.*

FUN! WELL, WE'D LOVE TO STAY AND HELP, BUT WE'VE GOTTA FIND A WOOD-AND-STEEL-FUSING TOOL.

FRED'S GOT ONE.

I WAS SITTING ON IT.

I WAS SITTING NEXT TO IT.

FANTASTIC.

THANKS, GUYS. HAVE A GOOD FUTURE.

MEANWHILE...

Flynn-Fletcher Antiques

MOM, YOU'VE GOT TO COME WITH ME *RIGHT NOW.*

I CAN'T, DEAR, I'M GETTING READY FOR MY TOUR. IT'S MY COMEBACK, COMEBACK, COMEBACK, COMEBACK, COMEBACK, COMEBACK--

--COMEBACK TOUR. TWO MORE COMEBACK TOURS AND I GET A *FREE PIE.*

OH, *COME ON!*

BACK AT THE MUSEUM...

MUSEUM OF NATURAL HISTORY

THAT'S FUNNY. WHAT HAPPENED TO--?

ZZAPP!

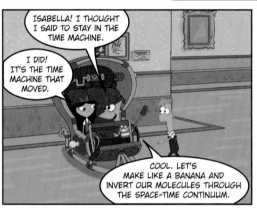

ISABELLA! I THOUGHT I SAID TO STAY IN THE TIME MACHINE.

I DID! IT'S THE TIME MACHINE THAT MOVED.

COOL. LET'S MAKE LIKE A BANANA AND INVERT OUR MOLECULES THROUGH THE SPACE-TIME CONTINUUM.

THEY WEREN'T AT MY HOUSE, SO THEY *MUST* BE HERE.

HONEY, I CAN'T MOVE AS FAST AS I USED TO.

ZZAPP!

THERE! NO! *WAIT!*

WE'RE TOO LATE!

MOM!

I'VE ALWAYS LOVED THIS OLD BONE.

MOM, YOU NEVER SAW THEM, AND YOU *STILL* NEVER SEE THEM.

IT'S NOT FAIR. IT'S NOT FAIR! *IT'S NOT FAIR!*

CANDACE, YOU'RE A GROWN WOMAN. I REALLY THOUGHT YOU HAD FINALLY MOVED PAST ALL THIS NONSENSE.

AT THE SAME TIME, TWENTY YEARS EARLIER...

COME ON, MOM, *HURRY!*

MUSEUM OF NATURAL HIST...

IN HERE. *SEE?* THE TIME MACHINE IS GONE.

ZZAPP!

OH, HI, CANDACE.

MOM!

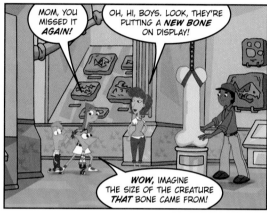

MOM, YOU MISSED IT *AGAIN!*

OH, HI, BOYS. LOOK, THEY'RE PUTTING A *NEW BONE* ON DISPLAY!

WOW, IMAGINE THE SIZE OF THE CREATURE *THAT* BONE CAME FROM!

STOMP!

NO! CAN'T YOU SEE? THEY WERE *TIME TRAVELING!*

CANDACE, THIS OBSESSION WITH THE BOYS HAS GONE ON *TOO* LONG. YOU NEED TO STOP.

I *WON'T* STOP! NEVER, NEVER, *NEVER!*

IN THE FUTURE...

AND I WAS *SO CLOSE* TO BUSTING THEM.

ZZAPP!

GREAT BERTHA'S BLOOMERS! I'VE **DONE** IT. I, PROFESSOR ONASSIS, HAVE INVENTED A **TIME MACHINE.**

EXCUSE ME, FUTURE FEMALE OF THE SPECIES, HAVE CORN DOGS BEEN INVENTED YET?

UM, YES.

HOT DOG! I'M **STAYING!**

AT CANDACE'S HOUSE IN THE FUTURE...

OKAY, SO SHARON'S INTERNET TOOTH POPS OUT **RIGHT** IN THE MIDDLE OF MATH CLASS-- WAIT, MY MOM'S CALLING.

HI, MOM. WHAT'S THE FIZZ?

AMANDA, I'M TAKING A SHORT TRIP TODAY.

WHILE I'M AWAY, YOU'RE IN CHARGE.

XAVIER! FRED! I'M IN CHARGE! WAIT--WHAT ARE YOU DOING?

NOTHING!

I **KNEW** IT! YOU NEVER DO **ANYTHING!**

NOW, WHERE DO I **GO**? OR MORE IMPORTANTLY, **WHEN**?

I KNOW. I'LL SET IT FOR A DATE I **KNOW** I CAN BUST THE BOYS! BACK TO THE FIRST DAY OF THAT SUMMER. THE DAY THEY BUILT THE **ROLLER COASTER.**

ZZAPP!

SOMETIMES IT'S **HERE**, SOMETIMES IT'S **NOT**. WHAT DO I CARE?

AND SO, ON THE FIRST DAY OF SUMMER TWENTY YEARS EARLIER...

MOM AND I SHOULD BE IN THE SUPERMARKET AT THIS EXACT MOMENT!

PHINEAS AND FERB GOT A *ROLLER COASTER?* YOU THINK WE GET A DISCOUNT IF WE BRING THE FLYER?

MAYBE WE'D BETTER TAKE IT.

HERE! LOOK, LOOK, LOOK! *SEE?* I TOLD YOU I'M NOT CRAZY. I *TOLD* YOU.

AND YOU'RE NOT CRAZY BECAUSE...?

AAAAAHH--!!!

THE POSTER'S MISSING, RIGHT?

FOLLOW ME!

OH, MY STARS! PHINEAS AND FERB MADE *THAT?* IT'S HORRIBLY UNSAFE AND DANGEROUS.

HELLO?

POLICE! FIRE DEPARTMENT! ARMY! AIR FORCE! MARINES!

ANYONE!

SAVE MY SONS!

NEARBY, *AGENT P* IS FOILING DOOFENSHMIRTZ'S PLAN TO HALT THE EARTH'S ROTATION WITH HIS *MAGNETISM MAGNIFIER...*

IT'S NO USE! IT'S NO USE! WE ARE *DOOMED!*

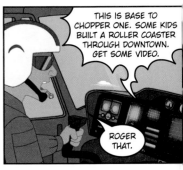

THIS IS BASE TO CHOPPER ONE. SOME KIDS BUILT A ROLLER COASTER THROUGH DOWNTOWN. GET SOME VIDEO.

ROGER THAT.

AGENT P ATTEMPTS TO LATCH ON TO THE HELICOPTER.

POOMF

MISS!

?

!

WITH 80 PERCENT OF THE COUNTRY'S TINFOIL HURTLING TOWARD HIM, AGENT P HAS ONLY A MOMENT TO ACT BEFORE--

CRUNCH!

I'M ALIVE!

BACK AT THE ROLLER COASTER...

ROGER. GOT THE KIDS. BRINGING 'EM DOWN NOW.

PHINEAS! FERB! YOU TWO ARE IN *SO* MUCH TROUBLE.

YES! YES!

MY WORK HERE IS DONE.

FUTURE CANDACE RETURNS TO THE MUSEUM...

MUSEUM OF NATURAL HISTORY

BACK TO THE FUTURE.

ZZAPP!

FIRST DAY ON THE JOB, AND I'M ALREADY SEEING THINGS.

ZZAPP!

AH, THANK GOODNESS. IT'S GREAT TO BE BACK-- *HOME?*

WELCOME TO DANVILLE

WELCOME TO DANVILLE?

UH-OH.

I CAN'T BELIEVE *THIS* IS DANVILLE.

HELLO? WHAT HAPPENED TO THE MUSEUM?

DIDN'T YOU GET THE NEW *SHMIRTZ-MAIL?* IT'S THE NEW *DOOFEN LAW.* LAW NUMBER SIX MILLION AND SEVEN: ALL MUSEUMS THAT AREN'T ABOUT DOOFENSHMIRTZ ARE TO BE DISMANTLED AND EXHIBITS TAKEN TO THE CITY DUMP.

HEY. WHY AREN'T YOU WEARING YOUR *LAB COAT?*

UH, I GOTTA GO SEE MY CHILDREN.

CHILDREN? THERE ARE NO CHILDREN ALLOWED ANYMORE.

HOW LONG HAVE I BEEN AWAY?

JOE'S STORE

JOE'S SIGNS

JOE'S STUFF

JOE

THAT'S STRANGE. JOE'S, JOE'S, JOE'S, JOE'S...

WHY IS EVERYONE NAMED *JOE?*

WHY ELSE? SO *EMPEROR DOOFENSHMIRTZ* NEED NOT BOTHER REMEMBERING NAMES.

AND WHO IS--

JOE'S STORE

JOE'S STUFF

JOL SIG

AT THE REMAINS OF THE DANVILLE LIBRARY...

THAT'S ODD. I'VE *GOT* TO FIND OUT WHAT HAPPENED IN THE PAST TWENTY YEARS.

YEAR ·20·19·18·17·

beep!

"OUR GLORIOUS DYSTOPIA BEGAN ONE SUMMER AFTERNOON WHEN *TWO LOCAL BOYS* WERE CAUGHT BUILDING AND RIDING A *DANGEROUS* ROLLER COASTER. THE RIGHTFUL REACTION BY CONCERNED PARENTS' GROUPS WAS TO STOP *ALL* CREATIVITY IN YOUNG PEOPLE BEFORE SOMEONE GOT HURT. EVERYTHING *FUN* AND *UNIQUE* WAS GLEEFULLY BANNED!"

"COLORING BOOKS WERE COLORED IN AHEAD OF TIME AND *INSIDE* THE LINES. EVENTUALLY, CHILDREN *THEMSELVES* WERE CHILDPROOFED AND STORED AWAY UNTIL ADULTHOOD. YES, OPPRESSIVE BEAUTY AND HAPPINESS WERE GRATEFULLY REPLACED BY THE *GLIMMERING CESSPOOL* WE WALLOW IN TODAY."

"A DEMORALIZED TRI-STATE AREA CRIED OUT TO BE OPPRESSED, AND THAT CRY WAS ANSWERED BY ONE HERO... *EMPEROR DOOFENSHMIRTZ!*"

AH, GET BACK TO WORK!

SO, THIS IS ALL *MY* FAULT! I'VE GOTTA STOP THIS!

EXCUSE ME, JOE. LAB COATS MUST BE WORN AT *ALL* TIMES.

I'VE GOT TO GO BACK IN TIME AGAIN AND UNDO WHAT I'VE DONE!

THE TIME MACHINE HAS PROBABLY BEEN TAKEN TO THE CITY DUMP BY NOW...

vvrt!

SIR! A WOMAN JUST RAN PAST YOUR STATUE WITHOUT BASKING IN YOUR AWFUL GLORY!

AH, JOE, YOU'RE SUCH A TATTLE-TALE.

UH, YEAH, THAT'S MY JOB DESCRIPTION: TATTLETALE.

QUIET! I NEED TO CHECK IN WITH AN OLD FRENEMY OF MINE...

AGENT P, ANOTHER FAILED MISSION. IT'S GOTTEN REALLY HARD TO DEFEAT DOOFENSHMIRTZ EVER SINCE WE SWORE THAT OATH TO OBEY HIM.

MAJOR MONOGRAM! I'VE DETECTED A TEMPORAL ANOMALY IN QUADRANT FOUR, WHICH MEANS A TIME MACHINE WAS RECENTLY USED THERE.

THAT'S IT! AGENT P! YOU'VE GOT TO GET TO THAT TIME MACHINE AND GO BACK TO THE PAST, RIGHT BEFORE THAT GIANT TINFOIL BALL PUT YOU IN A FULL-BODY CAST FOR EIGHTEEN MONTHS.

THAT'S WHEN DOOFENSHMIRTZ GOT THE UPPER HAND, AND IT'S BEEN DOWNHILL EVER SINCE.

THIS IS OUR CHANCE TO FIX IT.

OH, WAIT. PERRY THE PLATYPUS, CHANGE OF PLANS. INSTEAD OF DOING THAT, DON'T. ALL RIGHT. SEE YOU LATER.

REMEMBER THE OATH.

CURSE THAT OATH!

AHA! THERE IT IS!

BACK TO THE PAST. BACK TO THE PAST! **BACK TO THE PAST!**

ZZAPP!

BACK IN THE PAST...

ZZAPP!

NOW TO STOP MYSELF!

THERE I AM!

OOF!

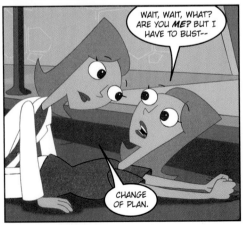

WAIT, WAIT, WHAT? ARE YOU *ME?* BUT I HAVE TO BUST--

CHANGE OF PLAN.

COME ON! I'LL EXPLAIN LATER! WE CAN'T LET CANDACE SEE US.

BUT *I'M* CANDACE!

SO AM I.

OH! OH! OH! OH! OH! MOM! **MOM!**

AWW! I WAS SO *CUTE!*

WHY DID YOU STOP ME? I WAS JUST ABOUT TO *BUST* THE BOYS!

THAT'S JUST IT. I'M FROM A FUTURE WHERE WE *DID* BUST THE BOYS.

REALLY? HOW WAS IT? WAS IT GREAT?

NO, IT WAS *AWFUL.* THE FUTURE GETS ALL MESSED UP--

OH, *LOOK!*

SO *THAT'S* HOW THAT HAPPENED.

LOOK, LOOK, LOOK, *SEE!*

OKAY, I GIVE UP. WHAT AM I SUPPOSED TO BE LOOKING AT?

PHINEAS, WE'RE FROM THE FUTURE. TWO *ALTERNATIVE* FUTURES. ONE THAT'S GOOD--

--AND ONE THAT'S TERRIBLE.

SOMEONE SHOULD REALLY FIX THAT.

WE DID!

SO, IF THE BAD FUTURE DOESN'T EXIST, SHOULDN'T THE CANDACE FROM THE BAD FUTURE CEASE TO EXIST TOO?

OH, DARN.

POP!

GUYS, I NEED YOUR HELP. THE TIME MACHINE I ARRIVED IN WAS SMASHED TO PIECES. I'M STUCK HERE UNLESS YOU GUYS CAN BUILD ME ONE.

FERB! ISN'T THERE AN OLD TIME MACHINE IN THE MUSEUM OF NATURAL HISTORY?

YES! THAT'S THE ONE YOU FIX LATER THIS SUMMER WHEN WE GO TO THE MUSEUM. IT'S THE ONE I TOOK BACK FROM THE FUTURE, BUT NOW IT'S DESTROYED.

OKAY. SO THE *FUTURE* TIME MACHINE GETS DESTROYED; THAT MEANS THE ONE HERE IN THE *PRESENT* IS RARIN' TO GO! WE'LL FIX IT, TAKE YOU TO THE FUTURE, BRING BACK THE TIME MACHINE, AND *UNFIX* IT AGAIN. SO, IT'LL BE READY TO BE FIXED WHEN WE GO TO THE MUSEUM THE *NEXT* TIME.

PHINEAS, I'M A FULLY GROWN WOMAN, AND I DIDN'T UNDERSTAND *ANY* OF THAT.

JUST TRUST ME. COME ON!

WAIT A MINUTE. WHAT'S GOING ON HERE?

I'D BETTER FOLLOW THEM...

AT THE MUSEUM...

MUSEUM OF NATURAL HISTORY

ARE YOU *SURE* YOU CAN FIX THIS TIME MACHINE?

DON'T WORRY, CANDACE. WE'RE ALMOST DONE.

CANDACE? TIME MACHINE?

AHA!

CANDACE, MEET CANDACE.

AWESOME! I *FINALLY* HAVE PROOF!

I'LL TAKE MY OLDER SELF, BRING HER TO MOM, MOM WILL SEE THE BOYS HAVE INVENTED SOME KIND OF TIME MACHINE, AND THEY'LL BE *BUSTED!*

OH, I *LOVE* YA, ME!

HA HA HA HA HA HA!!

COME ON, LET'S GO! LET'S GO SEE MOM! COME ON!

WOW, WAS I ALWAYS THIS NUTS?

CANDACE, HONEY, GET A HOLD OF YOURSELF. I HAVE NO INTEREST IN BUSTING THE BOYS ANYMORE.

WHAT? BUT YOU'RE ME! YOU HAVE TO WANT TO BUST THEM, BECAUSE I'M NEVER GONNA WANNA STOP BUSTING 'EM.

YA KNOW, SOMETIMES GETTING WHAT YOU WANT ISN'T WHAT YOU NEED. YOU'LL FIND OUT AS YOU MATURE.

COME ON, OLDER CANDACE! WE'RE READY!

CANDACE, JUST RELAX. EVERYTHING WORKS OUT.

TWENTY YEARS INTO THE FUTURE, HERE WE COME!

HA!

ZZZAPP!

AND SO, TWENTY YEARS INTO THE FUTURE YET AGAIN...

MUSEUM OF NATURAL HISTORY

AHA!

IF YOU WON'T SHOW *MY* MOM WHAT'S GOING ON, I'LL SHOW *YOUR* MOM! *I'M* ALL THE PROOF I NEED!

CANDACE! COME BACK!

WE'D BETTER GO AND GET HER. YOU KNOW THAT WHOLE *SPACE-TIME CONTINUUM* THING.

MOM AND DAD'S ANTIQUE STORE SHOULD STILL BE HERE.

YES! HERE IT IS!

Flynn-Fletcher Antiques

MOM, IT'S *ME*! CANDACE FROM THE *PAST*!

I CAME HERE IN A TIME MACHINE THAT PHINEAS AND FERB BORROWED FROM A MUSEUM!

YOU *GOTTA BUST THEM*!

HONEY, WHAT ARE YOU TALKING-- *CANDACE!* YOU'RE SO *YOUNG!*

MOM! YOU'RE SO OOOOOOOO--

--OOOOOOOO--

DON'T SAY IT.

YOU DON'T HAVE TO SAY THAT WORD. *I MEAN IT.*

--OOOLLLL--

MOM! YOU'RE SO *OLD!*

⇥*SIGH*⇤ HI, BOYS. AREN'T YOU A LITTLE YOUNG TO BE TIME TRAVELERS?

YES. YES, WE ARE.

A TIME MACHINE! ⇥*GASP*⇤ DOES THIS MEAN THAT *ALL* THOSE TIMES YOU TOLD ME THE BOYS WERE UP TO SOMETHING, THEY REALLY *WERE?*

YES, YES, YES!

OH, HONEY, I AM *SO* SORRY I DIDN'T BELIEVE YOU.

WOO-HOO! I FINALLY GOT THEM!

HELLOOOO? AREN'T YOU GOING TO *BUST* THEM?

ANDACE, **MY** PHINEAS AND FERB RE THIRTY YEARS OLD NOW. COULD CALL THEM, BUT PHINEAS S IN SWITZERLAND FOR THE WARDS CEREMONY AND FERB'S TILL AT CAMP DAVID. I DON'T HINK I HAVE JURISDICTION VER **THESE** GUYS NYMORE.

-:SIGH:-

OKAY, BUT OFFICIALLY, ON RECORD, THEY **ARE** BUSTED, RIGHT?

SURE, CANDACE. THEY'RE BUSTED.

YES!

EVERYONE HEADS BACK TO THE MUSEUM...

GUYS, WE'VE SEEN HOW TIME TRAVEL CAN MESS THINGS UP BIG TIME, SO **PROMISE** ME YOU WON'T GO INTO THE FUTURE AGAIN.

YEAH, MAYBE IT **IS** A BAD IDEA. JUST THINK, THIS ALL STARTED BECAUSE WE NEEDED A STEEL-AND-WOOD-FUSING TOOL.

HMM...

SNAP!

HEY, CANDACE, YOU NEVER TOLD US. HOW DO FERB AND I TURN OUT?

FANTASTIC. JUST KEEP DOING WHAT YOU'RE DOING. AND BE NICE TO YOUR SISTER.

YEAH. BE NICE TO YOUR SISTER.

YOU GUYS COMING OR WHAT?

HEY, WHERE'D YOU GET THAT SODA?

SO, THAT'S UNCLE PHINEAS AND FERB AS KIDS?

THAT'S RIGHT.

AND THAT GIRL LOOKS LIKE AUNT ISABELLA!

DID YA HEAR *THAT?* "AUNT ISABELLA." THAT MEANS I'M GONNA MARRY PHINEAS.

OR FERB.

~:KA-CHIK!:~

LET'S GO!

BYE!

ZZAPP!

~:SIGH:~ LOOKS LIKE EVERYTHING IS BACK TO NORMAL.

WOW, MOM, YOUR BROTHERS ARE *SO* COOL. MEANWHILE, I'M STUCK WITH-- *HEY,* WHERE'D THEY GO?

ZAP!

ZAP!

XAVIER AND FRED, **WHAT** ARE YOU DOING?

NOTHING.

SEE, MOM? THEY NEVER DO **ANYTHING.**

GIVE IT A REST, AMANDA.

AH, MEMORIES.

AND SO, IN THE PRESENT...

MUSEUM OF NATURAL HISTORY

OH, MAN, IN TWENTY YEARS, YOU GUYS ARE **SO** BUSTED!

I GUESS THAT'S A HOLLOW VICTORY. BUT IT PROVES YOU **CAN** BE BUSTED.

SO, I'M **NEVER** GONNA GIVE UP.

NEVER, NEVER, NEVER.

DID I SAY NEVER? YES, I DID.

NEVER, NEVER, NEVER. NEVER. NEVER. NEVER.

WELL, AT LEAST WE KNOW SHE MELLOWS WITH AGE.

LATER, IN THE BACKYARD...

YOU GOT TO HANG OUT WITH DINOSAURS?

YEAH, EARLIER THIS SUMMER.

HMPH!

WELL, *THANK YOU* FOR INVITING ME.

FERB, I KNOW WHAT WE'RE GONNA DO TODAY--

ZZAPP!

NO, YOU DON'T.

HERE'S THE WOOD-AND-STEEL-FUSING TOOL YOU NEED.

THANKS.

HEY, YOU WANT A SODA?

THANKS.

ZZAPP!

WELL, LOOKS LIKE WE DON'T HAVE TO GO TO THE FUTURE AFTER ALL.

SOME OTHER TIME, PERHAPS.

THE END!